SHADOWING THE WOLF-FACE REPTILES

DINOSAUR COVE™

DINOSAUR COVE™

SHADOWING THE WOLF-FACE REPTILES

by
REX STONE

illustrated by
MIKE SPOOR

Series created by
Working Partners Ltd

OXFORD
UNIVERSITY PRESS

Special thanks to Jan Burchett and Sara Vogler

For Tyler Rusinek-Graham, first of a new generation R.S.

This book is dedicated to Martin Saffery with
much gratitude and this particularly suitable title M.S.

OXFORD
UNIVERSITY PRESS

Great Clarendon Street, Oxford OX2 6DP
Oxford University Press is a department of the University of Oxford.
It furthers the University's objective of excellence in research, scholarship,
and education by publishing worldwide in

Oxford New York

Auckland Cape Town Dar es Salaam Hong Kong Karachi
Kuala Lumpur Madrid Melbourne Mexico City Nairobi
New Delhi Shanghai Taipei Toronto

With offices in

Argentina Austria Brazil Chile Czech Republic France Greece
Guatemala Hungary Italy Japan Poland Portugal Singapore
South Korea Switzerland Thailand Turkey Ukraine Vietnam

Oxford is a registered trade mark of Oxford University Press
in the UK and in certain other countries

© Working Partners Limited 2011
Illustrations © Mike Spoor 2011
Eye logo © Dominic Harman 2011

Series created by Working Partners Ltd
Dinosaur Cove is a registered trademark of Working Partners Ltd

The moral rights of the author have been asserted

Database right Oxford University Press (maker)

First published 2011

British Library Cataloguing in Publication Data

Data available

ISBN: 978-0-19-275629-9

1 3 5 7 9 10 8 6 4 2

Printed in Great Britain
Paper used in the production of this book is a natural,
recyclable product made from wood grown in sustainable forests
The manufacturing process conforms to the environmental
regulations of the country of origin

FACT FILE

➡️ JAMIE AND HIS BEST FRIEND, TOM, HAVE A SECRET—THEY'VE DISCOVERED A CAVE THAT LEADS THE WAY TO DINO WORLD! IF THE BOYS PLACE THEIR FEET INTO A SET OF FOSSILIZED DINOSAUR PRINTS, THEY'RE INSTANTLY TRANSPORTED TO AN ANCIENT LAND OF PREHISTORIC BEASTS. THE PERMIAN ERA SEEMS LIKE A GREAT PLACE TO TRY OUT THEIR WALKIE-TALKIES, BUT THE BOYS HAD BETTER NOT MAKE TOO MUCH NOISE . . .

JAMIE

- **FULL NAME:** JAMIE MORGAN
- **AGE:** 8 YEARS
- **SIZE:** 1 JATOM*
- **TOP SPEED:** 10 KPH
- **LIKES:** FOSSIL HUNTING AND LEARNING ABOUT DINOSAURS
- **DISLIKES:** BEING STUCK INDOORS

Jamie's eye

Jamie's foot

Jamie's hand

*NOTE: A JATOM IS THE SIZE OF JAMIE OR TOM: 125 CM TALL AND 27 KG IN WEIGHT

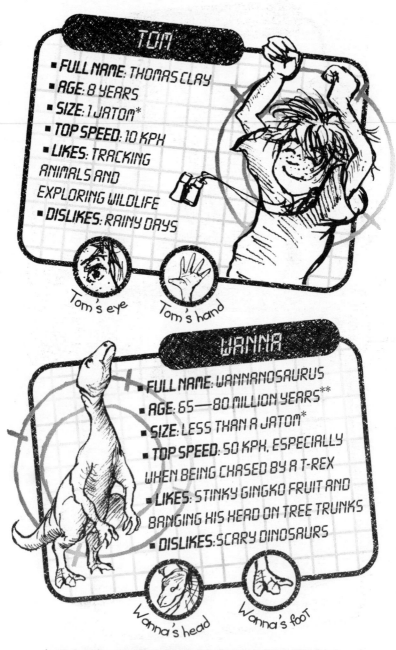

TOM

- **FULL NAME:** THOMAS CLAY
- **AGE:** 8 YEARS
- **SIZE:** 1 JATOM*
- **TOP SPEED:** 10 KPH
- **LIKES:** TRACKING ANIMALS AND EXPLORING WILDLIFE
- **DISLIKES:** RAINY DAYS

Tom's eye

Tom's hand

WANNA

- **FULL NAME:** WANNANOSAURUS
- **AGE:** 65—80 MILLION YEARS**
- **SIZE:** LESS THAN A JATOM*
- **TOP SPEED:** 50 KPH, ESPECIALLY WHEN BEING CHASED BY A T-REX
- **LIKES:** STINKY GINGKO FRUIT AND BANGING HIS HEAD ON TREE TRUNKS
- **DISLIKES:** SCARY DINOSAURS

Wanna's head

Wanna's foot

*NOTE: A JATOM IS THE SIZE OF JAMIE OR TOM: 125 CM TALL AND 27 KG IN WEIGHT
**NOTE: SCIENTISTS CALL THIS PERIOD THE LATE CRETACEOUS

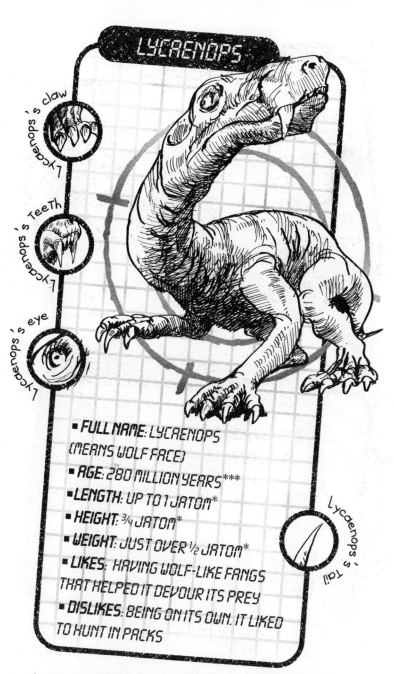

LYCAENOPS

Lycaenops's claw

Lycaenops's teeth

Lycaenops's eye

Lycaenops's tail

- **FULL NAME:** LYCAENOPS
(MEANS WOLF FACE)
- **AGE:** 280 MILLION YEARS***
- **LENGTH:** UP TO 1 JATOM*
- **HEIGHT:** ¾ JATOM*
- **WEIGHT:** JUST OVER ½ JATOM*
- **LIKES:** HAVING WOLF-LIKE FANGS
THAT HELPED IT DEVOUR ITS PREY
- **DISLIKES:** BEING ON ITS OWN. IT LIKED
TO HUNT IN PACKS

*NOTE: A JATOM IS THE SIZE OF JAMIE OR TOM: 125 CM TALL AND 27 KG IN WEIGHT
***NOTE: SCIENTISTS CALL THIS PERIOD THE PERMIAN

DINOSAUR COVE

Village

Marina

Sealight Head

8

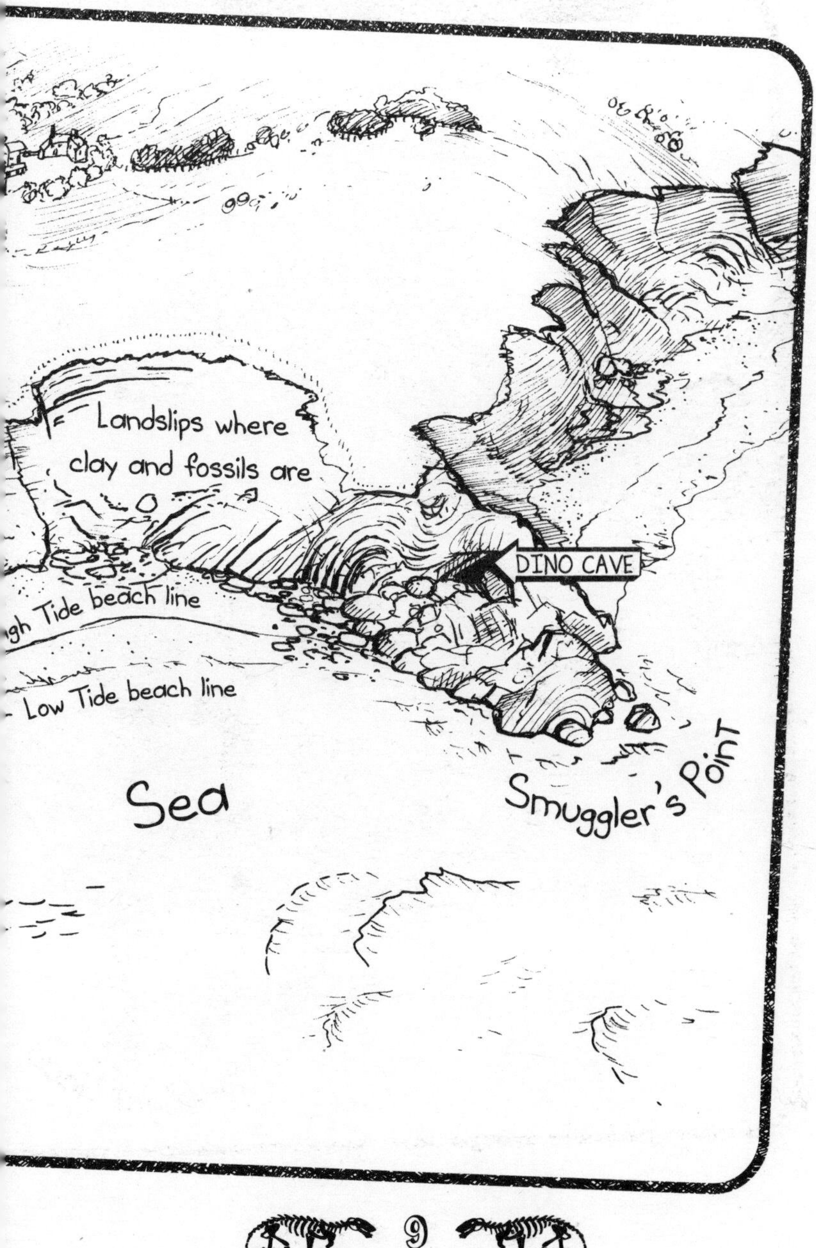

Landslips where clay and fossils are

DINO CAVE

High Tide beach line

Low Tide beach line

Sea

Smuggler's Point

Wheep!

Jamie Morgan nearly dropped his walkie-talkie as it screeched in his ear. He looked across the garden of his lighthouse home, searching for his best friend Tom Clay.

That bush is shaking, he thought, *and there's no wind.* He knew what that meant.

He crept over and was about to pounce when Tom's grinning face appeared through the leaves. 'BOO!' he said. Tom twiddled

the dial on his own walkie-talkie and Jamie's
shrieked again.

'Very funny!' said Jamie. 'I can make mine
louder than that.'

He turned the volume to full and an ear-
piercing wail filled the air.

Just then the back door opened and Jamie's
grandad stepped out, carrying a tray of plants.

Jamie and Tom ducked out of sight.

Boo!

'Target in view,' whispered Jamie. 'Let's give him a surprise. He's heading for the shed. You go round the water butt and I'll go round the roses.'

Using the cover of the flowerbed, Jamie crawled silently after Grandad. Tom disappeared behind the water butt.

But Grandad suddenly veered off the path.

'Alert! Target diverting to greenhouse,' Jamie muttered into his walkie-talkie.

'Roger that,' came Tom's reply. 'Meet you there.'

As Grandad fumbled for the greenhouse door, the boys crept up at him from both sides.

13

'Now!' hissed Jamie and they both twisted their dials.

Wheeep!

Grandad jumped and nearly dropped his plants. Then he spotted the boys and gave a beaming smile.

'Cheeky monkeys!' he said. 'Can't you find something better to spy on than an old fogey like me?' He went off into the greenhouse, chuckling.

Jamie's and Tom's eyes lit up.

'Are you thinking what I'm thinking?' Jamie whispered.

'A spy mission to Dino World!' Tom whispered back.

Jamie and Tom had a wonderful secret. Deep inside the cliffs of Dinosaur Cove they'd discovered the entrance to a prehistoric world. All they had to do was borrow a fossil from the dino museum in the lighthouse to make the magic work.

'Let's go back to the Permian age.' Jamie darted inside and was soon back carrying a trilobite. He dropped into his backpack. 'I've got my Fossil Finder,' he said. 'Anything else?'

'Don't forget these.' Tom added the walkie-talkies. 'We might need them.'

'Race you to the smugglers' cave,' said Jamie.

They dashed down to the beach and sprinted across the sand to the cliff on the other side. Scrambling up the boulders of Smuggler's Point, they were soon inside the dark old cave.

'Beat you!' yelled Tom as he squeezed through the little gap and into the hidden chamber at the back.

Jamie followed and placed his feet in the fossilized dinosaur footprints on the floor. 'Ready?' He stepped forward, Tom close behind. 'One, two, three, four …five.'

Flash!

They found themselves in
the dark underground cavern
back in the Permian age.
Following the light above,
they climbed the chimney-
like passage and pulled
themselves out to stand at
the entrance. Behind them
rose the steep sides of the old
volcano. At once, they felt
themselves gasp in the hot,
dry air.

'It's very quiet,' said
Jamie. 'Not a single creature
anywhere.'

'Do you think Wanna's
here?' Tom shaded his eyes
and peered up the mountain
slope behind them,

searching for the little wannanosaurus who always came with them on their adventures.

'Wanna!' called Jamie. 'Wanna?'

Grunk!

A small creature with a hard, domed head came bounding between the rocks and crashed into them. He licked their hands with his rasping tongue.

'Great to see you, Wanna!' exclaimed Tom. The little dino nosed at Jamie's backpack. 'I know what you're after,' said Jamie. 'But you'll have to be patient. I haven't had time to pick you any gingko treats yet.' Wanna impatiently stuck his nose into the backpack again, and this time the two walkie-talkies tumbled out.

'Maybe we should hook these to our shorts so we can talk all the time,' said Tom.

'Good idea,' said Jamie, as he grabbed one and attached it.

'Let's go and check out the view,' said Tom. 'We haven't seen much of this land yet.'

They walked away from the volcano slopes and scrambled up on to a flat boulder. In front of them lay the hot, dry desert and the sea beyond, sparkling in the sunshine. A thick steamy vapour rose from the swamp and drifted towards the tops of the forest trees.

'Look,' said Jamie,
gazing up the volcano slope
behind them. 'See that dark thing
moving along the rocks.'

Tom squinted in the bright sunshine.
'That's the inostrancevia that tried to eat
us last time we were here.'

Grunk!

Wanna froze beside them, his head on
one side. He gave a small whimper.

'What's the matter, boy?' asked Tom.
'The inostie is too far away to be a danger.
What have you picked up?'

'I can't see anything,' said Jamie, scanning
the view for a glimpse of some Permian
creatures.

Wanna whipped his head anxiously round.
He flattened himself on the smooth rock.

Then the boys heard it too. Pounding feet.
And they were coming closer.

'What's that?' whispered Jamie.

'I don't know,' said Tom. 'But Wanna's
not happy.'

SCRAWK!

An earsplitting screech filled the air.

'Down!' hissed Jamie. 'Something tells me
we have to get out of sight—right now!'

The boys threw themselves down on the rock. And just in time. A brown-striped creature went charging by, squealing and thrashing its tail in alarm.

'What's that?' exclaimed Tom, peeping over the edge. 'It looks like a big monitor lizard.'

'Varanops!' whispered Jamie, motioning for the frightened Wanna to stay behind the rock and out of sight. 'Dad's got a picture in the museum.'

A volley of high-pitched screeches filled
the air and at once a pack of long-snouted
reptiles came swarming after the varanops.

'No wonder the varra's scared!' said Tom.
'It's running for its life!'

'Poor varra,' said Jamie,
as they watched from above.
'I wouldn't want to be chased
by those creatures either. Look
at their sharp teeth. And their
long legs are built for speed. In fact
they remind me of a pack of wolves.'

The varanops darted left, straight into
the path of a large boulder that it couldn't
get round. At once it was surrounded by its
pursuers, snarling and snapping their sharp
teeth.

'It doesn't stand a chance,' muttered Tom.
Below them Wanna was whimpering quietly.
'What are those things?'

Jamie turned on his Fossil Finder. The
words '*HAPPY HUNTING*' appeared on
the screen. He tapped
in the newcomers'
characteristics.
'*LONG LEGS, SLENDER
SNOUTS, LARGE FANGS
ON UPPER AND LOWER
JAWS . . .*'

'*LYCAENOPS*,' read Tom.

'*PRONOUNCED
LY-SEE-NOPS.* You were right.

It says here that the shape of the skull and the fangs were similar to wolves today. And they hunted in packs like wolves do.'

The ly-sees were surging forwards, growling ferociously. The varra tried to scramble up the boulder, its claws scraping on the stone. But one of the pack leapt up and grabbed it round the neck, its long, sharp teeth clamping its victim like a vice. The others closed in.

The varanops screeched with anger and crashed around, thrashing in the ly-see's grip.

'It's fighting back!' exclaimed Tom.

With a whip of its neck, the varanops flung off its attacker.

The ly-see hurtled through the air and cannoned into the rest of the pack, sending them sprawling.

As they scrambled to their feet the varra saw its chance. It darted between them and sped off into the forest.

'It's got a head start,' exclaimed Tom.

Wanna seemed to sense what was happening and perked up.

Jamie stared at the ly-sees. They had only taken a couple of steps after the creature before they flopped down to the ground, panting heavily in the hot air. 'It doesn't need one,' he said. 'They're not chasing it.'

Tom held his walkie-talkie to his mouth and used it as a pretend microphone. 'And here on the Permian Plain, we see the lycaenops taking a rest after a hunt.'

Jamie grinned at him. Tom wanted to be a wildlife reporter when he grew up and he grabbed every chance to practise.

'Why have they given up so easily? Something isn't right,' Tom went on in his television voice. He grabbed his binoculars from around his neck and put them to his eyes. He gave a low whistle. Hooking his walkie-talkie onto his shorts, he turned to Jamie. In a serious voice, he said, 'I think I know why. They're exhausted.'

A young ly-see nudged one of the adults with its head, making a whining noise

like a pup. The adult nuzzled against it, then laid its head down on its front legs, its eyes half-closed.

Tom handed the binoculars to Jamie.

'Wow! They're really thin,' Jamie gasped in alarm. 'Their ribs are sticking out. That baby was after food. They're all starving.'

'Then we have to help them,' said Tom. 'Let's get a bit closer.'

'Better keep out of sight,' warned Jamie, as he handed the binoculars back to Tom. 'They

may be weak but we don't know what they'll do if they feel threatened.'

The boys climbed down from the rock quietly and gave Wanna a reassuring pet.

Darting for cover between the ferns, they crept through the red dust towards the ly-see pack. Wanna shuffled along on his belly, wagging his long, thin tail.

'Wanna thinks it's a game!' whispered Jamie. 'He's copying us.'

Tom grinned. 'Clever Wanna.'

An adult ly-see got to its feet. It had a jagged purple scar on the side of its face and gave a snarl, baring its long fangs.

The boys froze.

'We forgot to check the wind direction,' hissed Jamie. 'It's got our scent!'

CHAPTER 3

The scar-faced ly-see threw back its head.

Haroooooooooooooo!

It gave a long, desolate howl. The other ly-sees struggled to their feet too, howling and snapping their teeth.

Haroooooooooo!
Haroooooooooo!

'They really are like wolves,' Tom hissed back. 'That one with the scar must be the

Harooooooooo!

pack leader.
Let's get out
of range.'
They
moved away
until the
pack was calm
again. The
scar-faced ly-see
flopped to the ground,
panting, and the others
did the same.

'I've got an idea,' said
Jamie. 'They may be too weak
to find food but we're not.
Let's get them some dinner.'
He checked his Fossil Finder.
'Let's see . . . Ly-sees are
carnivores and mostly eat
small vertebrates.'

'That's an awesome mission,' declared Tom. 'I reckon the forest is the place to look. And I don't think that lot will be going far while we're gone.'

Skirting round the panting pack, they reached the pines and fern-like trees of the forest.

Huge flies droned past, flitting from leaf to leaf, and they could hear hoarse cries from distant creatures in the forest. Wanna nosed

about in the dust,
found a pine cone,
and began to crunch.

'Glad you've got
something to eat,' said
Jamie. 'But we mustn't
forget the poor ly-sees.
On with the search!'

Wanna suddenly
stared intently into the forest
trees, bits of forgotten cone falling from
his mouth.

Gr-runk!

'He sounds scared,' said Jamie. 'What's the matter, boy? What can you hear?'

Then the boys heard it too. A rustling sound—and it was getting closer.

'Something's coming,' gasped Tom.

They could see a creature stalking towards them. It was as big as a crocodile, with a low, ridged sail on its back. It raised its head, opened its mouth, and gave a deep roar.

'It's a sphenacodon—a carnivore,' said Tom hoarsely. 'Check out those teeth.'

'Let's get out of sight,' whispered Jamie.

They crept behind a lycopod tree. Wanna pushed between them, shivering.

'We won't let it hurt you,' murmured Tom, stroking his hard, domed head.

They peered nervously round the thick trunk and watched the powerful predator stomping through the undergrowth, looking this way and that for its next meal. Then it stopped and sniffed the air.

Roooaaarrrr!

The sphenacodon gave a deafening cry and began to charge.

'It's coming right for us!' said Jamie urgently.

GRUNK!

Wanna tore away from the boys and galloped off, panting in terror.

'He's got the right idea!' yelled Jamie. **'Run for it!'**

They took to their heels, leaping over ferns and ducking under low-hanging branches as they tried to escape the charging predator.

But the crashing footsteps grew louder as the sphenie gained on them.

Tom pushed his way through a curtain

of hanging vines. With horror, he felt his toe catch in a creeper. Before he could save himself he went sprawling.

ROAAARR!

Tom turned to see a flash of razor-sharp teeth. He flung himself aside, just in time—the sphenie's slavering jaws snapped shut behind him. He could feel the heat of its stinking breath on his back. He leapt to his feet, stumbling after Jamie.

But the sphenie was still pounding along in pursuit.

'Make for those rocks!' Jamie shouted over his shoulder.

Tom glanced up. There was a clearing

ahead. Wanna's tail was just disappearing into a dark hole between a pile of huge boulders. He saw Jamie dash across the clearing and dive into the narrow gap in the rocks.

'If I don't make it, I'm sphenie lunch!' Tom muttered to himself. His legs felt like lead and his lungs were bursting. The thunderous footsteps were getting closer.

'Look out, Tom!' he heard Jamie yell.

The sphenie was over him now, opening his jaws!

Tom only had seconds to act before he would be devoured by the sphenie. But what could he do?

An idea shot into Tom's head. He grabbed the walkie-talkie on his belt, fumbled for the dial and turned it on full blast.

WHEEP!

The sphenie's eyes grew wide with fear at the ear-splitting sound. It roared in terror— and Tom had his chance!

He flung himself into the gap where Jamie and Wanna were.

'Oomph!' gasped Jamie as Tom crashed on top of him.

43

The sphenie was still roaring outside, so Tom turned the dial again. The horrific, high-pitched sound was too much for the sphenie. Shaking its head madly from side to side it heaved its heavy body round and charged off. They heard it crashing away through the distant undergrowth, screeching as it went.

'Sorry about that,' panted Tom. 'Thanks for the soft landing!'

'Happy to help.' Jamie gave a grin. 'It's not every day we escape a sphenacodon!'

Wanna rushed out into the clearing and gave an angry *grunk* at its retreating back.

The boys crawled out from their hiding place. 'Anyone would think it was Wanna who'd seen off the sphenie,' said Tom, laughing.

grunk!

Wanna soon forgot the sphenie and started scampering round the boulders, snout to the ground.

Grunk! Grunk!

'What's he up to?' asked Tom.

'Wanna is
playing chase with
something.' Jamie took a
closer look.

A mass of green-and-yellow-striped
creatures were scuttling about at his feet.
'He's found a lizards' nest,' he told Tom.
'The sphenie must have uncovered them
with its enormous feet.'

Tom sat bolt upright and watched their
dino friend scamper about after the little
wriggling creatures. 'Just the thing for starving
ly-sees,' he declared. 'The lizards would make
a perfect meal.'

'But how are we going to get them to the
ly-sees?' asked Jamie. 'We can't very well put
them in our pockets. They'll all escape before
we reach the ly-sees.'

'You're right.' Tom looked thoughtful.
Then he jumped to his feet. 'Got it!' he cried.

'If we can't deliver their meal, they'll have to come here and get it.'

'Awesome plan!' said Jamie. 'We can herd them here. Remember how they got our scent? We can split up on either side of the pack and guide them here.'

'Fantastic idea!' exclaimed Tom. 'And we can use our walkie-talkies to stay in touch. Now we just have to find the way back to them.'

Wanna had left his game and was exploring among the trees. He stopped and gave a grunk.

'What's he heard?' muttered Jamie. 'Is the sphenie on its way again?'

The boys listened hard. 'No pounding footsteps!' whispered Tom after a while.

48

'A beast that size couldn't exactly creep up on us. I think we're safe.'

Wanna was moving stealthily through the forest.

'Come on, Wanna,' called Jamie. 'There's no time for exploring. We're playing hunt the ly-sees.'

But the little wannanosaurus took no notice. He was trotting quickly along now.

'Better go after him,' said Jamie. 'He might get lost.'

'Agreed,' said Tom. 'But we must be able to find our way back to the lizards.' He looked about them. 'See this conifer by the boulders? It sticks up above the others. Once we've caught up with Wanna and found the ly-sees, we just need to drive them back towards it and we'll find the lizards' nest again.'

The boys dashed after Wanna as he scampered through the forest. Gradually the trees thinned and the plains opened out in front of them. The little dino stopped, his head on one side.

Tom spotted a group of small creatures just beyond the edge of the trees. He caught Jamie's arm. 'We've come round in a circle,' he said. 'Wanna's led us just where we wanted to go . . . '

'Back to the ly-sees!' finished Jamie. 'Well done, Wanna.'

Their dino friend ran around them, grunking happily.

The exhausted lycaenops were lying just where Jamie and Tom had left them. The pack leader raised its scarred head weakly as the boys approached.

'I'll go to the left of the pack and you go to the right,' said Jamie. 'We'll skirt round until they're between us and the forest.'

Tom gave him a thumbs up and set off.

Jamie pulled a gingko from a nearby tree and tossed it to their wannanosaurus friend.

'You come with me, Wanna. But be quiet. We don't want to startle the ly-sees in case they decide to attack.'

Wanna trotted eagerly after him, his mouth full of gingko.

'Plan going well,' Jamie whispered into his walkie-talkie. 'The pack's watching, but they're not moving.'

'Roger. Don't get too near,' Tom answered. 'We don't want them to think we're predators trying to stalk them. They're so hungry they might lash out suddenly if they feel threatened.'

Several ly-sees struggled to their feet. Jamie stopped dead as the little creatures stared suspiciously in his direction. He put a hand on Wanna's domed head.

Haroooooooo!

'Keep still, boy.' The scar-faced leader gave a low growl and Wanna darted behind Jamie in fear.

The ly-see tensed, its eyes like burning coals.

Haroooooooo!

Jamie gulped. 'It's about to attack!'

CHAPTER 5

Wanna gave a *grunk* of alarm as the ly-see tossed its head, strings of saliva trailing from its fangs.

Tom's voice crackled over the walkie-talkie. 'Behind you!'

Jamie spun round. A vine trailed down from the branches of one of the trees. In one swift movement, he dropped his walkie-talkie to the ground, and grabbed Wanna around the middle with one arm. With his free hand, he reached up as high as

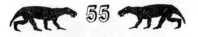

he could on the vine. He gripped it with his feet, shinnying up.

The furious ly-see gave another howl and charged in Jamie and Wanna's direction. It ran straight underneath the vine, then paused a few paces away.

Phew. It didn't see us, Jamie thought.

But his hand was sore from gripping the vine's rough surface, and his shoulder ached from holding Wanna. He let go of the vine. He and Wanna fell to the ground, and dived into a bush.

The ly-see turned. Its thin flanks heaved as it panted for breath. Then it saw something on the ground and padded over to it.

'The walkie-talkie,' Jamie muttered.

Harooooooooooo!

The ly-see howled into the walkie-talkie, flipping it about with its long snout.

'Pardon, Jamie?' said Tom's voice. 'I didn't quite catch that.'

'What a bonehead,' Jamie said to himself. 'Since when did I sound like a ly-see?'

The ly-see sniffed the walkie-talkie curiously, as if wondering where the strange noise was coming from. How would Jamie get it back?

Slurp!

Wanna still had the gingko he was chomping earlier. Gritting his teeth, Jamie pulled the stinky fruit away from him, a mixture of the smelly juice and Wanna's drool dripping down his arm.

As Wanna gave a *grunk* of annoyance, Jamie jumped out of the bush. He hurled the gingko past the ly-see, back into the clearing.

Harooooooooooooo!

The ly-see ran after it.

Jamie bent down and picked up his walkie-talkie. 'Phew,' he muttered to Tom. 'That was close.'

'What happened?' Tom asked.

'Tell you later,' Jamie replied. 'But we need to get the ly-sees to those lizards before they decide to eat us instead.'

Jamie walked slowly on until the ly-sees were between him and the forest. He was in the perfect place to start herding. 'Am in position now.'

'There's a load of rocks in my way here,' Tom replied. 'It'll take too long to skirt round them so I'm going across.'

Jamie could see Tom clambering over the jagged rocks. But all at once he saw his friend slip and heard him give a yell.

'Oh no!' gasped Jamie, as Tom tumbled on to the dry red sand, sending up clouds of dust.

The ly-sees' heads whipped round towards the sound. The scar-faced ly-see gave an angry howl, and the rest of the pack jumped to their feet. They fanned out into a semi-circle around the area where Tom lay in the dust.

'Run, Tom!' Jamie yelled into his walkie-talkie.

As Tom scrambled to his feet, the starving ly-sees charged.

Haroooooooooooooo! Haroooooooooooooo!

They howled, their jaws snapping. Tom ran, scrambling over the rocks, glancing behind as the pack drew nearer. The ly-see leader lurched at him, its fangs just missing Tom's arm.

Jamie's heart thudded. He had to do something—before the desperate ly-sees ate Tom!

CHAPTER 6

There was only one thing Jamie could do. He had to distract the ly-sees and give his friend a chance to escape.

He waved his arms and leapt in the air. 'Over here, ly-sees!' he bellowed.

Grunk!

Wanna was by his side.

'Ly-sees!' Jamie yelled again. 'This way!'

The creatures stopped and turned to stare at them, panting. Jamie's plan was working well. Too well. Now the ly-sees were creeping

towards them. The scar-faced
ly-see licked its lips.

'Run, Wanna!' Jamie
yelled. He sprinted for
the trees, the little dino
speeding ahead.

As he ran he risked a look
over his shoulder. The ly-sees
were following—and they
were running now.

Suddenly Jamie knew
just what to do. He and
Wanna would lead the
hungry creatures towards
the lizards' nest!

He quickly scanned the
treetops to find the tall
conifer that marked the
lizards' nest. There it was,
almost straight ahead. He

put a spurt on, but he could hear the ly-sees close behind, their breath rasping and their feet pounding the dusty earth. They were catching up with him.

Wanna was leading the way but now he skirted round to run at Jamie's side.

Grunk!

He seemed to be urging Jamie to go faster.

'I can't!' Jamie was panting for air now.

And then he saw the clearing. He was nearly there.

'This way, Wanna!' he yelled, making a mad dash for the pile of boulders. He threw himself among the rocks. Wanna squeezed in beside him.

'There's a chance they won't attack us if they spot the lizards,' he whispered.

He craned his neck to scan the ground.
'Trouble is—there's not a lizard in sight.'

Harooo! Harooo!

The ly-sees had arrived.
Jamie froze. Would they
be able to smell him
and Wanna? The
wolf-like creatures
were pacing around
the clearing.

They're searching for us,
he thought in alarm. *Any minute
now they'll get our scent.*

Haroooooooooo!

The ly-see leader pounced on a mound
of earth and at once green-and-yellow-
striped lizards spilled out, scurrying all over
the ground. Now the clearing was seething
with ly-sees jostling each other for food.

Jamie breathed a huge sigh of relief. The ly-sees had found the nest. They'd forgotten all about him and Wanna.

Jamie could hear a voice through his walkie-talkie. He lifted it up.

'Tom!' he whispered.

'Am I glad to hear you!' came Tom's voice. 'The last I saw, you had a pack of hungry ly-sees at your tail. I followed but I've lost you. All I can see is the pack eating something in the clearing. I was worried it was you two.'

Jamie peeped through a crack between the boulders. The ly-sees were still busily eating. 'We'll come and find you.'

Jamie and Wanna crept out from their rocky hiding place. Tom was waving to them from behind a nearby tree. Using the cover of the undergrowth, they slipped away to join him.

'That mission was a double success,' said Tom, as they huddled down to watch the pack eat their dinner. 'You saved me and you led the ly-sees to the lizards. They've got a lot more energy already.'

'Certainly have,' replied Jamie. 'The youngsters are even playing a game.'

The little ly-sees were tumbling around like puppies, snapping at their tails and rolling over in the dust.

'Time for us to go home,' said Tom.

They made their way back to the entrance of the underground cave.

'Bye, Wanna,' said Jamie. 'You must be hungry after all that excitement.' He picked a handful of gingkoes from a nearby tree and put them in a pile on the ground.

Grunk!

The little dinosaur settled down happily to eat his snack.

Jamie and Tom lowered themselves into the cave and placed their feet in the dino footprints. In an instant they were back in Dinosaur Cove.

As they climbed the cliff steps they saw Grandad coming out of the front door.

'I was just on my way to find you,' he called. 'Look what I've got here.' He held up two cans,

tied together by a long
piece of string.

'What is it?' asked Jamie.

'A walkie-talkie set!'
Grandad gave them a beaming
smile. 'I made it when I was a
lad. They were considered the latest
thing in secret communication for kids
then.' He thrust a tin each at the boys.
'You have to stand as far apart as you can
until the string's tight. Then take turns to
speak into your tin while the other one
listens. Try them out.'

Grandad watched
as the boys walked to
opposite ends of the garden.
When Jamie felt the pull on the
string he held the can over his
mouth. Tom put his to his ear.

'Dino explorer Jamie Morgan calling,' he whispered.

'Tom Stone here,' came Tom's voice, loud and clear through the can. 'Just returned safely from an awesome mission to the Permian.'

Jamie gave his grandad a thumbs up. 'They're great!' he called. 'Wouldn't have been any good for herding ly-sees, though,' he whispered into his can. 'And I've thought of something else.'

'What's that?' came Tom's reply.

'They don't make that horrible screech,' Jamie told him. 'We'd never be able to scare off a fierce sphenocodon! Over and out!'

Permian Sea

Desert

Pools of water

Swamp

Forest

Permian Sea

GLOSSARY

Cycads (si-kads) – plants with thick trunks, palm-like leaves and cones.

Gingko (gink-oh) – a tree native to China called a 'living fossil' because fossils of it have been found dating back millions of years, yet they are still around today. Also known as the stink bomb tree because of its smelly apricot-like fruit.

Inostrancevia (in-os-tran-see-vee-ah) – a large, predatory mammal-like reptile.

Lycaenops (ly-see-nops) – a dog-like reptile which hunted in packs. Its name means 'dog face'.

Lycopod (ly-koh-pod) – tree with leaves growing directly out of its trunk and branches. They fell off as the tree grew, leaving a cluster of leaves at the top.

Pareiasaur (par-ee-ah-sor) – a stocky, herbivorous reptile with bony skin and knobs on its skull. Some scientists think it might have evolved into a modern-day turtle.

Permian (per-mee-an) – The Permian period lasted from 290 to 248 million years ago. During this time the supercontinent Pangaea was formed and non-dinosaur reptiles roamed the earth.

Sphenacodon (sfee-nah-koh-don) – a carnivorous lizard living in wooded areas. It had a ridge on its back like a small sail.

Trilobite (try-loh-byt) – an extinct marine animal that had an outside skeleton divided into three parts.

Varanops (va-ran-ops) – a reptile that resembled an alligator.

Wannanosaurus (wah-nan-oh-sor-us) – a dinosaur that only ate plants and used its hard, flat skull to defend itself. Named after the place it was discovered: Wannano in China.

I'm about to be eaten!
You have to help me!